Come on an adventure with me and learn about my life in the jungle

TRUE TO LIFE BOOKS

Educating children about endangered animals.

Jan Latta author and wildlife photographer.

Hello, my name is Sleepy, and I'm a sloth. We live in the trees of the Central and South American tropical rainforests.

Sloths first appeared on earth over 35,000 million years ago.

I'm a **two-toed sloth** because I have two toes with claws on my front feet and three toes on my back feet.

And there are **three-toed sloths**. They have three toes with claws on their front and back feet.

I am a unique **mammal**
because I live upside down.

I can rotate my head just like an owl
and I move like a primate.

I have a stomach like a cow
and the body temperature of a snake.
Isn't that amazing!

I have very strong arms.

I can hold onto branches with my long claws when I'm hanging upside down.

Look at my claws.
They can grow up to 10 centimeters long.

I move very slowly and sleep for up to 10 hours a day to conserve my energy.

I curl into a ball to sleep in the fork of a tree, so I'm safe from predators.

Sloths are called **folivores**, which means we eat leaves, flowers, fruits, buds and shoots.

Sometimes our food takes a month to digest.

I especially like
hibiscus flowers.

Once a week I slowly climb down from my tree to the ground. I hold onto the tree trunk and with a funny wiggle-poo dance, I go to the toilet.

This helps to fertilise the ground so the sloth moths, who live in my hair, can lay their eggs in it.

When I walk on the ground it can be very dangerous.

My hair grows from my tummy to my back, so when it rains, the water just runs off.

Isn't that clever!

Sometimes I look green because **algae** grows in my hair.

This is a very good **camouflage**, especially if an eagle wants to attack me.

When I was a baby,
I lived with my mother for about eight months.

She taught me what foods to eat
and where to find special trees.

Say hello to my brother and sister.

They have fun climbing
through the jungle together.

I have a map of the forest
in my head and I can find my favourite leaves
just by smell.

My eyesight is not very good,
especially in strong sunlight.

And we smile, and smile, all the time.

SLOTH FACTS

The areas where sloths can be seen in the wild.

SCIENTIFIC NAME:
Sloths are mammals and classified in the families *Megalonychidae* and *Bradypodidae.* Scientific names: Bradypus and Venegatus
Order: *Pilosa*
Higher classification: *Folivora*

Bradypodidae three-toed sloths
Pygmy three-toed sloths *(Bradypus pygmaeus)*
Maned sloths *(Bradypus torquatus)*
Pale-throated sloths *(Bradypus tridactylus)*
Brown-throated sloths *(Bradypus variegatus)*

Megalonychidae two-toed sloths
Linnaeus's two-toed sloths *(Choloepus didactylus)*
Hoffmann's two-toed sloths *(Choloepus hoffmanni)*

HABITAT:
Sloths live in trees in the rainforests in Central and South America. They hang upside down to eat and sleep.

LENGTH:
The two-toed sloth is larger than the three-toed sloth and can grow up to 80 centimeters long.

WEIGHT:
The two-toed sloth can weigh up to 10 kilograms and the three-toed sloth can weigh up to 6 kilograms.

DIET:
Sloths eat leaves, fruit, buds and shoots.

PREDATORS:
Harpy eagles, jaguars, ocelots and snakes.

LIFESPAN:
The two-toed sloth can live up to 46 years and the three-toed sloth can live up to 30 years. They have a very important role in the tropical rainforest eco-system, but with deforestation, sloths will lose their habitat and food source.

DID YOU KNOW ?

- Megalonyx is the Greek name (meaning great claw) for the giant ground sloths. In 1797 Thomas Jefferson (the American Founding Father), named it when fossil specimens were found in a West Virginia cave.

- Paleontologists have identified 23 different kinds of fossils of prehistoric sloths. The largest was the Megatherium. It was seven meters tall and weighed seven tons.

- Megatherium means 'giant beast' in Latin. It lived from about 35 million to 11,000 years ago, coinciding with the last Ice Age.

- The pygmy three-toed sloth is the most endangered sloth. It is only found on a tiny island off the Panama Coast.

- Sloths don't sweat. This protects them from predators because sloths don't smell.

- Sloths can live upside down because their internal organs are fixed to their rib cage. This stops their organs weighing down on their lungs.

- Two-toed sloths can tilt their head back at 45° angles to look for food or danger while hanging upside down from a branch.

- Sloths are arboreal which means they live in the trees.

- The brown-throated sloth is the most common mid-sized mammal in the Central and the South American rainforests.

- The two-toed sloth is nocturnal and is more active at night, whereas the three-toed sloth is diurnal and active both during the day and at night..

- Sloths are related to the anteaters and the armadillos.

CREATING SLEEPY THE SLOTH BOOK

"To create this book, I travelled for three days from Australia to Dallas, in the USA. I then flew to San Jose in Costa Rica, then to a tiny airport called Limon, and finally down the coast, where I met Encar Garcia. Encar is a very special woman who has dedicated her life to helping injured animals, especially sloths, at the Jaguar Rescue Centre.

I've been researching sloths for five years. It was wonderful to be so close to these unique mammals. But, taking photographs was a challenge because sloths like to sleep for most of the day. I had to be very patient. With the help of Enca and her wonderful team, the photography was successful. I also created a video so that children can see the sloths moving very, very slowly in the trees.

Sloths smile all the time and I found myself always smiling back. After many exciting days I reluctantly had to leave, but I smiled all the way home."

Jan Latta, author and wildlife photographer.

Jan holding a rescued baby sloth.

Rescued babies in the nursery.

QUESTIONS

1. Where do sloths live?
2. How long have sloths been on earth?
3. What is unique about sloths?
4. Can sloths swim?
5. What do sloths eat?
6. What creatures live in the sloth's hair?
7. Where do sloths sleep at night?
8. What sounds do sloths make?
9. What is a herbivore?
10. What animals are sloths related to?

Can you help the moth find its home in the sloth's hair?

THOMAS HAMLYN-HARRIS

Have some fun creating and wearing animal masks!

On white felt, or heavy paper, draw the panda's eyes, nose and mouth. Glue on ears. Cut out holes for your eyes to see. Add black socks on your hands for paws. Then you can be a panda in a bamboo forest in China.

Cut out an oval shape on card-board and paint a sloth's face on it. Make holes for your eyes to see. Put on your mask, and move very, very, slowly, just like a sloth.

ORANGUTAN ORANGES

Make an orangutan face on an orange. Stick on sultanas for eyes and nose and draw on a smile. Use strips of orange paper for its long hair.

PAPER PAWS

Draw the shape of a leopard's paw on two paper bags and paint them yellow. Add big black leopard spots and claws with a black marker. Wear your fierce leopard paws!

Draw a **LEOPON** a cross between a female lioness and a male leopard. Have lots of fun with your imagination.

MEERKAT FINGER PUPPETS

Place two pieces of paper flat in front of you and put your forefinger on top. Draw around the outline of your finger and cut out the shape allowing at least a centimetre extra space. Staple the top and sides together keeping the bottom edges open. Draw the face, arms legs and add a tail.

CHEETAH WORD GAME

- How many words can you make out of the word cheetah?
- You should be able to make at least five words.
- Have fun looking at the letters. Try putting them in different sequences to find new words.

Draw a lion's face on thick yellow paper. Make holes for your eyes to see. Glue on ears and a paper mane. With a mighty roar, have fun wearing your lion's mask.

Paint large and small paper plates grey. Glue on ears and a big black nose. Draw a smiley mouth and make holes for your eyes to see. Pick gum leaves and branches and pretend to be a koala in the trees.

ANIMAL SUPERSTARS

Look for TV advertisements featuring wild animals. Why do you think that animal has been used for the ad.

GIRAFFE DOT DRAWING

Draw the outline of a giraffe on paper. Make a dot painting using brown, orange and yellow paint for its coat. Add the face, hooves and mane in black paint.

GUMLEAF PRINT

Collect gum leaves and make a paper rubbing of the leaves. Place a flattened leaf under a piece of paper and gently rub a crayon over the top, making sure you don't move the paper.

RHINO RESCUE

- Make a list of all the endangered rhinos in the world.
- How many are close to being extinct?
- How many have disappeared from earth?
- How many are critically endangered?
- What is happening to save them?

ANIMAL ANCESTORS

Research the names of animals that were alive during the Ice Age. A woolly ancestor of the elephant roamed the earth. What was its name? Draw its picture. Why did it become extinct?

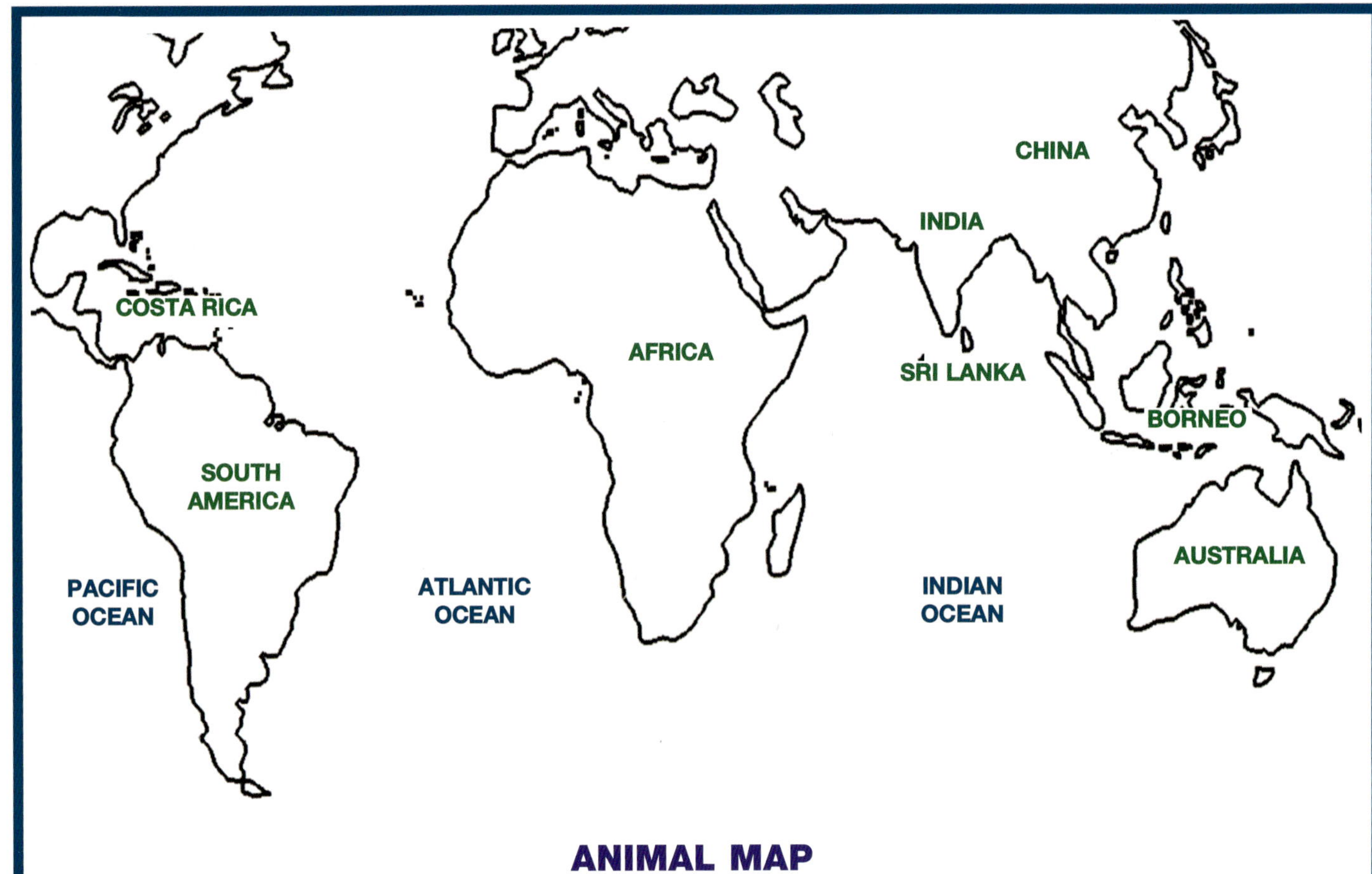

ANIMAL MAP

Find the countries on the map where the animals in the *True to Life Books* live in the wild. Add the animals and their habitats.

COLLECTIVE QUIZ

Some groups of animals are described using collective nouns. Here are some from the *True to Life Books*:

A journey of giraffes
A herd of elephants
A pod of hippos
A pride of lions
A crash of rhinos
A leap of leopards
A swift of tigers
A clan of hyenas
A litter of cubs
How many collective nouns for animals can you add?

DIARY OF A SAFARI

Write about your exciting safari adventures in Africa! Watch some of the videos www.truetolifebooks.com.au to inspire your creativity.

What animals might you see?
Where will you stop to camp?
Do you live in a tent?
Describe your guide.
What dangers might you face?
Will you see animals hunting?
How will you travel between camps?
What foods will you eat?
Will you be frightened at night?

colour in the sloth and the tree where it lives.

THOMAS HAMLYN-HARRIS

INTERESTING WEBSITES

GLOBIO www.globio.org

ANIMAL PLANET www.animalplanet.com/wild-animals/sloth/

KIDS' PLANET www.kidsplanet.org

NATIONAL GEOGRAPHIC KIDS www.nationalgeographic.com/sloth

WORLD WILDLIFE FUND www.worldwildlife.org/species/sloth

BBC SCIENCE AND WILDLIFE www.bbc.co.uk/nature/wildlife/factfiles

ANIMAL INFO www.animalinfo.org

SCIENCE KIDS www.sciencekids.co.nz/sciencefacts/animals/sloth.html

LIVE SCIENCE www.livescience.com

SLOTHVILLE www.slothville.com/what-is-a-sloth/

ANIMAL CORNER animalcorner.co.uk/animals/sloth/

DISCOVERY KIDS discoverykids.com/?s=sloth

HOW TO ADOPT A SLOTH

- The school or a class of caring students can adopt an animal from the **Jaguar Rescue Centre**.
- Donation is US$100 for one year and you can choose which animal you would like to adopt.
- You will receive a certificate, a photograph of your adopted animal, and updates about its progress throughout the year.
- You will also receive information and news about what's new in the rescue centre.
- Please send an email to ***info@jaguarrescue.foundation*** for more information.

See Sleepy the sloth video and exciting educational videos of wild animals from the True to Life Books on www.truetolifebooks.com.au